First Little Readers™ F

Cal the Cactus

by Liza Charlesworth

ISBN: 978-1-338-29797-3

Illustrated by Tammie Lyon

First printing, June 2018.

 Published by Scholastic Inc. Printed in Jiaxing, China.

Cal was a happy cactus,
who lived in the desert.

Cal had just one problem.
He was NOT good
at giving high fives.

He saw Rabbit.
"Hi buddy!" said Cal.
He gave Rabbit a high five.

"OUCH!" shouted Rabbit.
"I'm sorry," said Cal.

He saw Fox.
"Hi buddy!" said Cal.
He gave Fox a high five.

"OUCH!" shouted Fox.
"I'm sorry," said Cal.

He saw Owl.
"Hi buddy!" said Cal.
He gave Owl a high five.

"OUCH!" shouted Owl.
"I'm sorry," said Cal.

He saw Kangaroo.
"Hi buddy!" said Cal.
"I can't give you a high five."
"Why not?" asked Kangaroo.
"My hands are too prickly,"
said Cal sadly.

"Hmmmm," said Kangaroo.
"I have an idea."
Then off she hopped.

When Kangaroo came back,
she had a mitten on.
"Give me a high five," she said.

So Cal gave his buddy a high five.
"Awesome!" said Kangaroo.
The mitten worked!

Kangaroo gave mittens to
Rabbit and Fox and Owl, too.

Then Cal gave his desert buddies high fives all day . . .

and all night, too!